MAR 07

Masters of Mayhem

By Scott Ciencin
Based on the series created by
Bob Schooley and Mark McCorkle

New York

Printed in the United States of America

First Edition
1 3 5 7 9 10 8 6 4 2

Library of Congress Catalog Card Number: 2004114359

ISBN 0-7868-4689-5

For more Disney Press fun, visit www.disneybooks.com
Visit DisneyChannel.com

nacho, interrupted

"**I**t'll be naco-licious!" cries Ron Stoppable. "Vive el naco-lution!"

Kim Possible doubles over with good-natured laughter. She can't remember the last time her best bud was so excited.

Bueno Nacho's third annual "You Make the Sauce" competition is just hours away, and Ron has created a special hot sauce for "nacos," the nacho/taco combination he invented while working at Bueno Nacho.

Kim grins at her friend. "I thought you didn't like competitions."

"It's all about the spirit of the sauce," Ron says. "And it ends in the bliss of the big taste-for-all!"

Just then, the Kimmunicator chirps and Kim's friend, Wade, appears on-screen. "What's up, Wade?" Kim asks.

3

Turn to the next page.

"Check it out," Wade says. Suddenly, the small Kimmunicator screen splits into images of Professor Dementor, Motor Ed, Jackie the Jackal, and Gill. "I picked up this crazy video feed online," explains Wade. "Four of your worst enemies are up to major badness—*and* they're broadcasting their every move to one other."

"Weird," observes Kim. "Why would they do that?"

"Sounds like they got into a fight over who's the baddest bad guy of them all. So they're having a contest. Whoever wins gets the title 'Master of Mayhem.'"

"And no matter which of them wins, the whole *world* loses," says Kim.

Behind her, Ron is still focused on nacos, and tries to get his pet mole rat, Rufus, to try the sauce.

Kim grabs Ron and explains the sitch. She expects him to be bummed because he might miss the big hot-sauce competition. Instead, he just smiles.

"Hel-*lo*?" cries Ron. "If you need me, K.P., I'm there. The Ronness is ready to rumble!"

Now it's up to *you*. Go to the next page to help Kim decide which villain she'll tackle first.

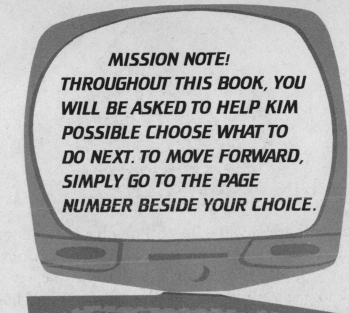

MISSION NOTE!
THROUGHOUT THIS BOOK, YOU
WILL BE ASKED TO HELP KIM
POSSIBLE CHOOSE WHAT TO
DO NEXT. TO MOVE FORWARD,
SIMPLY GO TO THE PAGE
NUMBER BESIDE YOUR CHOICE.

Which of Kim's archenemies should she go after? It's time for *you* to help Kim pick a villain!

 To throw down with Jackie the Jackal, turn to page 7.

 To begin the race of your life with Motor Ed, turn to page 23.

 To face underwater excitement with Gill, turn to page 44.

 To rock out with Professor Dementor, turn to page 74.

Hey, there! Wade here! I'm checking in to remind you not to read this book like you normally would. Do NOT turn to the next page. Go back to page 5 and pick a villain for Kim and her friends to battle, then flip to the page number beside your choice and begin to read. As you read, you will be asked to make choices for Kim and her friends. These choices will send you to different pages all over the book. What happens to Kim and her friends will depend on your choices. If you come to a dead end, don't get tweaked. Just keep starting the book until you have helped Kim defeat all of the villains! There are tons of different endings, so you can read this book over and over and it will always be different. Ready? Okay, time to pick a villain!

JACKIE THE JACKAL

The sun blazes high in the sky as Kim makes her way through a swirling desert sandstorm in Egypt. Ron trudges behind her.

"The only thing hotter than this place is my trusty supersecret naco sauce," Ron observes as he adjusts his goggles. "Speaking of which, can we move this along so I can get back home in time for the contest?"

Rufus, Ron's pet mole rat, peers up from his backpack and nods as he wipes the sweat from his forehead.

Kim grasps her Kimmunicator and squints at the screen. Wade shouts over the howling winds, "Almost there, K.P.!"

Suddenly, the winds die down and Kim is standing before a magnificent ancient Egyptian city. Pyramids rise around her and stone sphinxes sneer in the distance.

7

Turn to the next page.

"Whoa," says Kim.

"Yup—pretty much what every scientist in the world said when satellites showed the city rising from the sands this morning," agrees Wade. "This city has been buried for centuries. Put that together with the theft two weeks ago of the Amulet of Anubis and robberies of other Egyptian artifacts rumored to have magical powers, and it's pretty clear that Jackie the Jackal is making a comeback!"

Kim taps the sand from her goggles. "Security footage of a giant jackal-headed guy stealing the stuff didn't hurt either."

The city appears to be deserted. Kim, Ron, and Rufus walk through its streets while Wade monitors the weather patterns and energy levels. He is picking up weird energy fluctuations

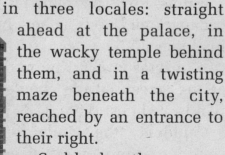

in three locales: straight ahead at the palace, in the wacky temple behind them, and in a twisting maze beneath the city, reached by an entrance to their right.

Suddenly, the energy readings go off the charts—

8

Go to the next page.

directly where Kim, Ron, and Rufus are standing. Kim whirls as strange tripodlike devices burst from the sand. Their glowing green eyes stare at the trio of newcomers. The devices unleash a torrent of weird lights on Kim, Ron, and Rufus. When the lights fade, all three find themselves transformed.

Kim looks down to see that she is wearing a crazy wrestling outfit. She starts to point at something and a lightning bolt shoots out of her index finger, scorching a patch of sand. Meanwhile, Ron has developed massive arms and has a punch that can break through walls. And Rufus is able to change his body into either stone or steel.

"This is Rontastic!" boasts Ron. "I'm like a superhero! I'm gonna call myself Roundhouse Ron." He points to his pet mole rat. "You can be Rufus the Metamorphosing Mole Rat."

Uh-huh, uh-huh, agrees the excited Rufus.

"And K.P., I'm going to go with Lightning Kim for you," Ron declares.

Kim frowns. "Yeah, that's great Ron. But

Turn to the next page.

why were we given these powers?"

As if to answer her question, the tripod devices start to hum again. A huge holographic image of Jackie the Jackal's face appears.

"You're in for something special today, fight fans!" Jackie promises as he welcomes his viewers. "We're counting down to the world premiere of Jackie the Jackal's All-Star Wrasslin' Extravaganza, which will be broadcast to every TV set in the world!"

"These fighters aren't just anyone," Jackie continues. "They're you. That's right, tonight you'll see ordinary people from every walk of life transformed into lean, mean, super-powered fighting machines. Who will prove themselves worthy of a one-on-one, winner-take-all brawl with the one and only Jackie the Jackal? Stay tuned to find out."

The tripods shut down and sink back into the ground.

"Wade, is Jackie broadcasting some sort of show?" Kim asks.

10

Go to the next page.

"Yeah," says Wade, "and the ratings are through the roof. He may have the whole world watching. There's some sort of hypnotic signal built into the broadcast so that once people start watching it, they can't stop. Jackie's going to take over the world with this show—unless you can stop him."

Wade tells Kim that the energy readings he picked up earlier are even stronger now. It's up to you to help Kim decide what to do next.

🌐 **Turn to page 36 to look for Jackie the Jackal in the palace.**

🌐 **Turn to page 61 to walk down a tunnel and search the ancient temple.**

🌐 **Turn to page 73 to navigate the twisting maze.**

Kim races ahead. She spots Motor Ed. He's perched on top of the Road Hog, cackling wildly.

"You think you can stop me with that bucket of bolts?" he cries to Kim, flipping his mullet. "I own this road, and soon I'll own them all. Seriously!"

Motor Ed pours on the heat, unleashing a ray gun from the rear of the Road Hog that turns patches of the road into fiery molten magma. Kim maneuvers through the obstacle course carefully.

"This is just like Ultimate Road Race 2999!" cries Ron. "The special-edition video game, natch."

What is Ron babbling about? Kim thinks. Then she nods as an idea strikes her.

🌐 **Turn to page 32 if Kim should take on the obstacle course herself.**

🌐 **Turn to page 59 if Kim should let Ron drive.**

Kim, Ron, and Rufus lead the hammerhead guards away from the compound. The three friends slice through the water, propellant tanks giving them power. As they navigate a network of twisting underwater chasms, the snapping maws of the hammer- heads close in.

Suddenly, up ahead, a narrow tunnel branches to the right and to the left. Kim sees a weird glow off to the right. Maybe it's another way into the compound. To the left, there is only darkness.

🌐 **Turn to page 26 if Kim should go toward the light.**

🌐 **Turn to page 77 to send Kim into the darkness.**

Kim pulls out her compact and brilliant light comes out, temporarily blinding the crowd as Kim races for the stage using her high-tech sonar.

Rmmmm-rmmmm-bddda-bddda-bddd-da-BOOOM!

The music blaring from the stage disrupts the sonar. Running blind, Kim bounces into one group of angry fans, stumbles, and is squished between panicked concertgoers. The singers spring from the stage, tear Kim's, Ron's, and Rufus's gear from them, and all three become part of Dementor's mind-controlled legion!

👎 **Don't be tweaked! Turn to page 74 for another chance to stop the evil Professor Dementor.**

*T*he 4-D Dude reels under Rufus's attack. Rufus switches from stone to steel and back again. The energy generated by the changes in form scrambles 4-D Dude's powers.

"You're goin' down!" shouts Ron.

The Dude goes down—and Kim, Ron, and Rufus get a reward for winning the round: a path lights up, which guides them out of the maze and up into the great palace.

Within the palace, they soon face another challenge: a royal rumble. This time, a dozen opponents, including such wacky fighters as the Perilous Panda, beset the trio.

Though the odds are against them, Kim and her friends stand ready to fight—but it isn't necessary. Their show of bravery impresses Judge Jackie, and they're sent through a tunnel to their next match.

🌐 **Turn to page 61 to see where the tunnel comes out.**

Kim races ahead in a desperate attempt to stop Motor Ed and cut off his link to the Possibles' minivan. The obstacle course ahead of her grows more intense.

The Road Hog barrels along at breakneck speed, its great maw opening wide to swallow up other cars before spitting out a hailstorm of steel, glass, and plastic debris at Kim.

"And I thought the Tweebs were messy!" says Kim.

"Yo, Red, how about I shake things up?" asks Motor Ed. He pulls out ahead of Kim and hits a switch that causes the road to buckle as if an earthquake were striking.

16

Go to the next page.

"Now I know how a basketball feels!" Ron hollers as the Smart Car bounces all over the place. But Kim stays calm and rides out the attack.

"Great thinking, K.P.!" Wade says. "Motor Ed had to put so much energy into creating the earthquake hazards that he cut his link to the Possible minivan. Your family's safe!"

Kim concentrates on the road. The Road Hog is zipping off to her right. No, wait, there it is sailing off to the left, *too*.

Now there are two of them!

"One of them is an illusion," says Wade. "But I can't get a lock on which one is real."

A tollbooth rises up in the distance just as the road forks.

🌐 **Turn to page 12 if Kim should go after the Road Hog to her right.**

🌐 **Turn to page 41 if Kim should follow the Road Hog to her left.**

Johnny leads Kim, Ron, and Rufus to the turncoat scientists—and knocks Kim out without warning. Ron and Rufus leap at Johnny, but he jams a weird device against Kim's side and hollers, "Back off, hero-boy, or your pal gets it!"

Suddenly, Johnny seems to be changing into someone else . . . Gill! He'd been using an image distorter, too.

"I only saved you three from the other patrol so you'd trust me," declares Gill. "Now the rebels have seen that I can't be defeated, and no one's left to stand in my way."

He summons the Fish Patrol and the captured trio is taken away. Way harsh!

☞ **You lose. Turn to page 44 to get back in the water with Gill.**

Kim shakes the small vial of hot sauce, pops the cork, and unleashes the crimson liquid on the Ice Queen. The reaction generates so much steam, the trio can't see more than a few inches ahead.

"See?" says Kim. "She's nothing but hot air!"

"Badical!" says Ron.

Kim, Ron, and Rufus start toward the door—or where they think the door is. But the steam makes it hard to see, so Ron runs into a shelf of cat sculptures. "Wow," he says. "I saw a show about ancient Egyptian sculpture on the Culture Channel." He picks up one of the sculptures and the shelf moves, revealing a secret passageway.

"The Ronness has saved the day again," he says.

Kim rolls her eyes and follows Ron into the secret tunnel.

🌐 **Where will the tunnel come out? Turn to page 61 to find out.**

Kim can't deny that the boys of Romeo Five are all that—and she's banking that each of these girls has a favorite.

"We all know that one of the Romeos is way cuter than the others," Kim teases. "You girls know which one I'm talking about!"

"It's Trey," says Lisa.

"No way, it's so totally J.T.," Millie counters.

"As if. Kevin could be a male model," Marie says.

While the girls continue to argue, Kim, Ron, and Rufus slip past them and head outside toward the bus. When they reach the bus and creep inside, they find Dementor manipulating his crazy mind-control mechanisms. He laughs when he sees Kim and the others.

"What's so funny?" asks Kim.

Dementor gestures at the scene outside the bus's windows: legions of mind-controlled teens surround the bus. There is no escape!

"I've summoned help, Possible!" rants

Go to the next page.

Dementor. "Now you'll see the true meaning of mayhem!"

Ron gulps. "Wouldn't it be less painful to just look it up in the dictionary?"

Then something strange happens—the teens attack the bus, knocking it onto its side.

"Wait!" cries Dementor. "I gave no such command! There must be some sort of system malfunction."

He types furiously and suddenly the bus is moved upright again.

No matter, Kim and her friends aren't going to be able to escape the angry mob. Looks like Dementor wins.

🖐 **So not the drama! Turn to page 74 to make Professor Dementor sing a different tune.**

Kim decides to send Rufus in. Rufus turns to rock as he squares off against Lizard Girl.

Lizard Girl's tail sweeps the mole rat's legs out from under him. She easily gets him in a viselike hold. But because he is stone, she cannot inject him with her knockout venom.

Turning his fists to steel, Rufus clocks Lizard Girl. She's down for the count.

"Bon diggity!" shouts Ron.

"And the winner is . . . Rufus the Metamophosing Mole Rat!" booms Jackie's voice. "And now it's time for the Ultimate Grudge Match—against me."

🌐 **Turn to page 52 to go toe-to-toe with Jackie the Jackal.**

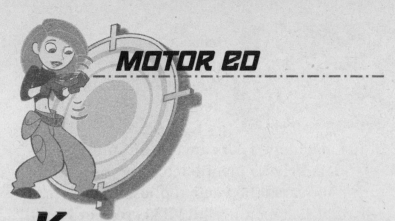

MOTOR ED

"**K**im, are you sure this is a good idea?" asks Ron as he clutches his seat belt. The wind from the open window whips through his hair as Kim drives her Smart Car down the highway. They zigzag between abandoned, smashed, and overturned cars. The road is littered with moon-like craters. Debris crunches and snaps under their tires.

"You know it, Ron," cries Kim. "Wade's wiggin'—and so am I."

Wade had picked up close to a hundred major distress calls from the highway—including one from the Possible minivan. Wade's face appears on a screen emerging from the Smart Car's dashboard.

"I have a satellite confirmation," states Wade. "Motor Ed is up to some way-dangerous

Turn to the next page.

 tricks. You should be seeing him any second now. Wherever he goes, mayhem follows!"

Ron points out that all of the abandoned cars are still running.

"Some drivers mentioned they just couldn't turn their cars off," Wade replies. "I don't know why that's happening, but I'll keep an eye on it."

Kim catches up to Motor Ed—who is riding atop a high-speed vehicle with the words ROAD HOG stenciled on the side. The Road Hog is one part Humvee, one part robot dinosaur, and it moves fast as lightning. Motor Ed is wearing a weird control helmet above his mullet.

Kim is about to take on the crazed motorhead, when she notices the Possible car in hot pursuit. Or so it seems. Then she sees that her mom, who is in the driver's seat, doesn't have her hands on the wheel, and her dad is frantically flipping through the car's manual as if it might explain how the car is driving itself. In the back, the Tweebs are trying to use their own gadgetry to take control of the car.

"Hey, Red, what do you think of my ride?" calls Motor Ed. "You're looking at the crowning

24

Go to the next page.

achievement of my scientific genius. See, that's not smoke the Road Hog is spitting out! Those are nanospores—tiny computers that attach themselves to anything with a motor and let me take control. You must have some sort of special shield on that car. I'll figure that out later—after I trash it!"

Motor Ed laughs. "All I have to do is hit maximum speed with the Road Hog here and it'll create enough spores to cover the world and let me take control of anything and everything  with wheels. Then you'll *really* see some motorized mayhem!"

With that he blazes ahead while sending the Possibles' car in the other direction to a road filled with deadly hazards!

🌐 **Turn to page 16 if Kim should chase Motor Ed.**

🌐 **Turn to page 53 if Kim should go after the Possible car.**

*T*he bright glow looms. Kim zooms toward it, using the last of her propellant—and bursts into the center of a beautiful underwater light show. Strange, dazzling, part-human creatures surround her, swinging their electric eel–like arms and legs at her. Uh-oh. More guards!

"Sorry, my dance card is full," says Kim as she tries to pull away from the stinging limbs.

It's no use. Kim is zapped and so are Ron and Rufus. The guards take them to Gill, who keeps them prisoner until he completes his plan to flood the world with mutant-creating waters.

👎 **Glub, glub! Turn to page 44 to try to hook Gill again.**

Kim decides to battle Jackie alone. She's finally mastered her lightning abilities. She fires bolts of lightning all around, distracting Jackie.

When he's least expecting it, Kim uses her powers to cut the chain on the Amulet of Anubis. It falls to the ground and smashes to pieces. There is a great explosion and Jackie is suddenly no longer a jackal-headed giant. He's back to his short, crabby, human self. The cameras disappear and the broadcast stops. Everyone's powers fade, and the city starts to sink into the ground.

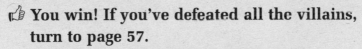

Everything goes back to normal. Now if only Ron can get back to the sauce contest in time!

👍 **You win! If you've defeated all the villains, turn to page 57.**

👍 **To pick a new villain, turn to page 5.**

"Boys, you might want to apply some more hair gel," Kim says to the band members as she takes out a mirror and pretends to check her own 'do.

The singers rush over, grab the mirror, and fight over who gets to check their perfect looks first. Rufus is just about to grab their mind-control gear when the crazed crowd rushes the stage, overwhelming Kim, Ron, and Rufus.

"Make room, make room!" a loud voice booms. Wearing his own protective gear, Dementor takes the stage with more of his henchmen, easily capturing Kim and her friends and forcing her to watch as the chaos he's begun at the concert hall spills out to the town beyond.

"I am the master of mayhem!" he proclaims.

☞ Turn to page 74 for another shot at teaching the professor a lesson.

Ron dives off the rigging into the crowd below. Kim follows.

"Stage dive!" hollers Ron.

The concert-crazed teens see them coming and open their arms, catching the pair. The Pop Ninjas leap after them, but the band has just commanded the concert-goers to dance, so no one is paying attention.

Smack!

The Ninjas land, moaning and nursing headaches that will keep them out of Kim's hair for quite some time.

"Well, I guess they got the beat after all," observes Ron. "The downbeat that is!"

🌐 **It's all gravy, baby! Turn to page 72 to take on the band.**

Kim hurls her boomerang hair comb at the 4-D Dude. It bounces off the wall beside 4-D's head and pings off every surface in sight. He ducks and spins away from the wildly whipping weapon—and Ron moves in with his roundhouse right!

And passes through 4-D.

"Puh-leese!" 4-D Dude hollers, racing deeper into the darkness.

Kim, Ron, and Rufus chase after him. A dead end looms. Then 4-D races through a wall and disappears. Behind them, a heavy stone door slides into place.

They're trapped!

☞ **No big! Turn to page 7 for another shot at Jackie the Jackal.**

Kim hands Ron her Kimmunicator and he climbs up to a skylight. He pops it open and crawls onto the roof so he can get a connection to Wade.

"Dude, we need some help here," Ron says. "Anything you can do?"

"I'll just work on a new signal, one that will override Dementor's," Wade replies. He types furiously, then hits one last key and sits back, looking pleased.

Ron looks down into the arena. The crowd seems to have snapped out of it.

"Bon diggity!" cries Ron in triumph.

Inside, Dementor's face suddenly appears on the huge video panels. "I command you to go forth and create chaos! I am the master of mayhem, and I command you!" he says desperately.

The teens realize that Dementor has been controlling them. They flood from the stadium and chase after his tour bus. The day is saved!

👍 You win! If you've defeated all the villains, turn to page 57.

👍 To pick a new villain, turn to page 5.

Kim decides to keep driving. But she hits a patch of lava and the Smart Car's rubber tires burst into flames. Kim grapples with the steer-

ing wheel, but the rims start to melt. Then the engine rebels and she skids to a stop on the side of the road. The lava flows around the car and suddenly cools, turning to rock. She's trapped!

👎 **Bummer, dude. Turn to page 23 for another try at Motor Ed.**

Seeing Kim, Ron, and Rufus leap back to the Smart Car gives the driver of a news van the courage to come closer—to try to get exclusive footage. Unfortunately, the exhaust from his car gives the Road Hog the boost it needs to race ahead in a blur and take control of the roadway.

Motor Ed wins!

☞ **Turn to page 23 to race after Motor Ed again.**

Kim, Ron, Rufus, and Johnny follow the markings and step inside Gill's inner sanctum. It's deserted. Johnny hits a button, sealing them in.

"Johnny" taps his belt buckle. His face crackles and changes, revealing . . . Gill!

"I thought I could count on you guys," Gill

grouses. "Now I'll have to come up with another way to break the spirit of the rebels."

Gill leaves and posts guards outside the door. All seems lost—but Ron smiles and produces the image distorter. "When in a fish tank . . ."

In seconds, guards hurry to the door, responding to urgent cries—and see a group of fellow mutants who say they were tricked into taking the place of the prisoners. The guards enter—and Kim Calamari knocks them out.

Flounder Ron leads the trio to the nerve center of the complex by following the strange symbols on the wall. They burst in on Gill, who is

34

Go to the next page.

just about to activate a rocket that will take his giant "transforming ray" machine to the nearest ocean.

Ron and Rufus go after Gill, so Kim can deal with the rocket. But Gill quickly gets the upper hand and is about to plunge Ron into a vat of mondo-mutant–inducing waters.

🌐 **Turn to page 64 if Kim should help Ron.**

🌐 **Turn to page 67 if Kim should disarm the rocket.**

Kim, Ron, and Rufus enter the palace. Frowning, Kim smacks the side of her Kimmunicator.

"Trouble?" asks Ron.

Kim shrugs. "It's dead. We won't be able to contact Wade."

Turning a corner, they reach a vast din- ing hall—and are met with a sudden chill in the air. Straight ahead, a breathtaking ice sculp- ture of an ancient goddess glimmers. Suddenly, the sculpture moves—and stares straight at Kim, Ron, and Rufus!

Just then, a battalion of small, round, floating camera droids arrives.

"Welcome, fight fans!" roars the unseen Jackie from a speaker in the wall. "She's as cold as ice and *twice* as deadly! Give it up for the Ice Queen!"

Raising her hands, the Ice Queen sends a bar- rage of razor-sharp icicles at Kim and her crew.

"I guess we're on Jackie's TV wrestling show," Kim remarks.

Go to the next page.

"I'm all over it!" says Ron, ready for his star turn.

Ron smashes the icicles, while Kim's electrical fingers go wild and nearly singe Rufus.

"My bad," Kim says to the cowering mole rat. "I never was very good at bolting."

Undeterred, the Ice Queen presses closer, hurling frozen boulders at the beleaguered trio.

As the Ice Queen approaches, Ron gets a closer look at her. "She may be as cold as ice, K.P., but she's a total hottie!"

Just then, Kim spots Ten-Alarm Naco Sauce sticking out of Ron's pocket.

A gleam comes into Kim's eyes. "Let's see how hot she really is." She snatches the vial of hot sauce from her bud.

Kim wants to use Ron's hot sauce on the Ice Queen. But Ron thinks they've got a better shot if they launch one attack using all of their powers.

☻ Turn to page 19 to see if the Ice Queen can take the heat.

☻ Turn to page 56 to see if three heads really are better than one.

"Boo-ya!" Ron yells again as he rips out the wires— but it proves to be a bad decision. Those wires were there to help Motor Ed control the complex machinery onboard his crazy vehicle.

The gauges, as well as all of the Road Hog's functions, fire up simultaneously. The car runs wild, shaking Motor Ed loose and destroying everything in its path.

It's maximum overdrive—and maximum mayhem!

☞ **Turn to page 23 to go after Motor Ed again.**

*J*ohnny follows Kim, Ron, and Rufus into the abandoned engineering room. Ron hits all four of them with the image distorter. Kim, Ron, and Rufus suddenly look like fish folk. "Johnny" flickers and fizzles—and disappears, leaving Gill in his place.

"You guys are too easy!" Gill bellows. "Johnny" was Gill in disguise all along. Using the image distorter on him had removed his image.

The Fish Patrol rushes in. Gill produces another device: he explains that this one enables him to take the special talents of the last person he aims at. He'd pointed it at a cool camp counselor to become the suave, funny, brilliant Johnny Seven.

Ron frowns. "Yeah, well, how *else* could you have managed it?"

Gill aims the device at Kim—but Ron leaps in front of her. The beam hits Ron, and bright light bounces back to Gill.

"Nachos . . . tacos . . . the hot

Turn to the next page.

sauce. So many ingredients, so little time!" cries Gill. He's become Ron!

"K.P.," Gill continues. "I've got to reverse the mutations and stop the rocket from melting the ice caps. And fast. There's a hot-sauce competition to go to."

Gill hits a button on the control panel to stop the rocket. Then he pulls another switch. The Fish Patrol changes back into the kids from the clown camp. Gill clutches his head, then so does Ron.

"I'm back, K.P.," Ron says.

The button has reversed all the mutations and personality changes!

"Not for long!" Gill replies. But Gill's too late. Ron jumps in front of the control panel, blocking Gill's access. With no mutant minions to back him  up, Kim captures Gill in no time and places a call to the police.

👍 **You win! If you've defeated all the villains, turn to page 57.**

👍 **To pick a new villain, turn to page 5.**

Kim races through the abandoned tollbooth after the Road Hog. When she comes out the other side, she no longer sees Motor Ed's crazy contraption. Uh-oh, she followed the illusion!

Suddenly, she's swarmed by dozens of cars with tinted windows. And every single one of them has the words MOTOR ED RULES spray-painted on its sides.

It was a trap!

They bang against the Smart Car and try to force Kim off the road.

Another car smashes into her—and Kim's Smart Car flips over onto its roof, the tires spinning helplessly in the air. Ed's fleet of cars surrounds her. Kim is trapped.

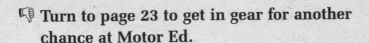

☞ **Turn to page 23 to get in gear for another chance at Motor Ed.**

Kim, Ron, and Rufus slip backstage. "Where do you think Dementor is, K.P.?"  Ron asks. Just then, Ron spots a door leading to the rear parking lot. Outside, the band's tour bus glows with strange and nefarious activity.

"That's got to be his lair!" Kim says. "Dementor, you are *so* busted."

Suddenly, a trio of crazed young female fans surges from the shadows and blocks the way out.

"I'm Lisa," announces the raven-haired girl in the lead. "And that's Millie and Marie. And unless you're a 'true fan,' you're not getting anywhere near that bus."

🌐 Yikes! Turn to page 20 for Kim to use her band knowledge to divide and conquer the crazed fans.

🌐 Woo-chow! Turn to page 58 if Kim should challenge the trio to a fashion slam.

ightning shoots from Kim's finger, forming a vast volleyball net.

"Uh . . . I don't think I like this game!" Budd hollers as the crackling net surrounds him. He's powerless to stop bouncing, and soon he hits the high-voltage net.

"Knockout!" Jackie crows as Budd goes down for the count. "You three are through to the next round."

A stone door opens, and the trio race to a huge courtyard, where they are waylaid by two more wrestlers—Giant Boy and Lizard Girl.

The fighting is hard and heavy, but soon Giant Boy and Lizard Girl are on the ropes. Kim decides she needs to focus her energy on one of her opponents. Should she ask Ron or Rufus to fight the other one?

🌐 **Turn to page 22 if Rufus should fight.**
🌐 **Turn to page 50 if Ron should fight.**

Kim, Ron, and Rufus leap from a school bus onto the damp earth of the vast woods surrounding Camp Wannaweep. They asked the driver to drop them here, instead of at home. Kim whirls to thank the driver for the ride, but the door hisses shut and the bus rockets down the road.

"Y'know, K.P., that guy might have the right idea," says Ron. He shudders as the entrance to the abandoned camp beckons, remembering the awful experience he and Kim had here during summer camp.

The Kimmunicator chirps. Kim answers it as she surveys the scene of Ron's worst nightmare ever. "What up, Wade?"

"Even more stories about the meltdown at the polar ice cap by those weird manphibian

Go to the next page.

creatures," reports Wade. "They're part-human, part-fish mutants that generate heat. Soldiers can't stop 'em, scientists can't explain 'em. It sounds fishy to me. And that means Gill!"

Kim nods. "And if Gill is behind this, he's sure to have set up his headquarters at Camp Wannaweep."

The camp appears deserted. Signs have been knocked down and tables are overturned. The same is true in the camps across the lake— the science camp, band camp, and clown camp. But weird shimmering lights appear on the surface of the lake.

"It's crazy," observes Ron. "Gill used chemicals from science camp runoff and then the swamp in order to turn into a fish boy. Now it looks like he poured his *own* chemicals into the lake. Maybe that's how he made the manphibians!"

Turn to the next page.

A sound captures their attention. Kim and her pals whirl to face a trio of science kids who have been transformed into Gill's favorite kinds of mutants: one is part frog, the other two are part salamander.

"The lake waters have created many mutations," one of the kids explains.

"Yeah, tell us something we *don't* know," says Ron.

"Okay," replies the leader. "Gill led an uprising here, promising students from every camp power unlike any we have ever known. All we had to do in return was swim in the weird toxic waters of the lake. That turned us into fish mutants. But the three of us were rejected—our hearts just weren't into being fish."

"Although, turning into giant bugs would have been *way* cool," argues one of his companions.

The fish scientists present Kim with a device they've been working on at their camp. "This is an image distorter," explains the leader. "It casts a field that will hide your true appearance and make you look like fish people."

The trio helps Kim and her friends outfit themselves in underwater gear that will protect

Go to the next page.

them from the murky, mutating waters. Then Kim, Ron, and Rufus plunge into the lake.

They swim deeper and deeper—until they get closer to the shimmering lights that were visible from the surface. The lights reveal the outline of a great domed compound. Whoa, these are some serious supervillain headquarters.

Kim swims around, looking for a way in. She finds one—just as a trio of hammerhead sharks finds her. No, wait, beneath the giant scary fish heads these guys have human bodies and carry weird high-tech gear. They must be Gill's guards!

🌐 Turn to page 13 if Kim should lead the guards away from the compound.

🌐 Turn to page 55 if Kim should lead Ron and Rufus into the compound.

Kim decides to have Ron and Rufus help her. Rufus, his body completely changed to steel, takes the lead. Jackie kicks him with a massive boot, sending him flying through the air at Ron.

Ron ducks as Rufus lands on the floor. Kim jumps on Jackie's back, but he shakes her off.

Then Ron moves in. Jackie ducks and dodges roundhouse punches, which fall on Kim by mistake. Ron gasps in shock, and Jackie clocks him.

This fight is over and Jackie's the winner. Now there's nothing left to stop him.

👎 **No big! Turn to page 7 to try your luck against Jackie the Jackal again.**

"I'm all over it, Wade. But first I've got to get my family," yells Kim. She pulls alongside her folks' minivan and motions for them to get into the Smart Car.

Once they do, the Smart Car announces that there are too many people in it. One of them has to bail in order for the car to make the jump.

Kim slaps on her jetpack backpack and jumps out just in time.

"Wade, do your stuff!" Kim cries into her Kimmunicator as she takes to the air. But Wade is already on it. He takes control of the Smart Car, making the jump safely as Kim flies behind it. Kim lands just as her folks and the Tweebs are getting out of the car.

"Again, again, again!" plead the Tweebs.

Kim dives back into the Smart Car and promises to come back as soon as she's stopped Motor Ed.

🌐 **Turn to page 12 to get back on Motor Ed's trail.**

Ron fights Giant Boy. The courtyard resounds with the riotous thunder of his round-house punches. Giant Boy is on the ropes in seconds! He starts to teeter.

"You know what they say," taunts Ron, "the bigger they are—hmm . . . I may have miscalculated. RUN!"

But it's too late. The giant falls on top of Kim, Ron, and Rufus.

"Now there is nothing any of you can do to stop me!" cackles the Jackal as the trio tries to break free.

And he's right—they're pinned!

👎 **All is not lost! Turn to page 7 for another shot at Jackie the Jackal.**

Kim, Ron, and Rufus take to the rigging high above. They spot the lighting and power grid and are about to shut the concert down when a group of men wearing stylish black suits and ponytails leaps onto the rigging and try to capture them.

"We're the Pop Ninjas," the nearest man announces. "Special agents to Professor Dementor. Come along quietly or we'll have to bust a move on you!"

"I'd *have* to be mind-controlled to want to see you guys dance," comments Kim.

Kim battles Dementor's stylish henchmen fiercely, but she's outnumbered.

"I've got a plan," calls Ron. "No time to explain. Just follow my lead."

☻ **Most badical! Turn to page 29 for Kim to back Ron's play.**

☻ **Turn to page 65 if Kim should cut the power.**

Kim, Ron, and Rufus follow one of Jackie's minions to the throne room. Torches surround a royal wrestling ring. Golden snakes and scarabs are everywhere. A pair of beautiful cat-headed women named Bast and Nast flank the jackal-headed giant.

"Welcome to the final round. You have three choices," Jackie says to Kim. The Amulet of Anubis, which gives Jackie his power, hangs from his neck. "You can fight me on your own. You can fight me with your two friends. Or you can pick any two fighters from the city to help."

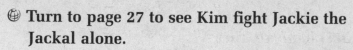

🌐 **Turn to page 27 to see Kim fight Jackie the Jackal alone.**

🌐 **Turn to page 48 to bring in Ron and Rufus.**

🌐 **Turn to page 71 to see Kim draft two other fighters.**

Kim puts the pedal to the metal and zooms after her family. Cars swerve toward them, and cars crash in front of them, creating obstacles.

Wade uses the Smart Car's remote capacities to enable Kim to patch into the G.P.S. communications system in her parents' minivan.

"Honey, we've regained some control over the steering, but we still can't stop the car!" calls Mom Possible.

"Guys, just do what I tell you," Kim says. "Cut the wheel right. Now left. Straighten out. A little to the right."

"This is like playing Twister behind the wheel!" her mom exclaims.

But it works. Both cars avoid the terrible dangers of the road.

Then they see a drawbridge up ahead that is being raised so a boat can pass through. The Possible minivan speeds up. It seems bound for the jump, no matter what they do.

"Kim!" calls Wade from the Kimmunicator.

Turn to the next page.

"You need to get to the other side of that bridge. From there I can get you on an intercept course back to Motor Ed!"

🌐 Turn to page 49 if Kim should try to transfer the Possibles to her Smart Car before making the jump.

🌐 Turn to page 63 if Kim should try to stop both cars before they reach the bridge.

*K*im, Ron, and Rufus slip inside the compound as the hammerhead guards sound the alarm. Ron points to the image distorters.

"Time to get fishy with it," Ron suggests.

Kim nods. They use the devices to make themselves look like fish people. The guards rush right past them—at first. Then they whirl and look back, sniffing loudly. These two may *look* fishy—but they don't *smell* fishy.

"Uh-oh," Ron whispers, "they're looking at us like we just got out of a sushi restaurant—and they want revenge."

The guards mob them. Kim and Ron are captured. Gill wins.

👎 **Oh well. Turn to page 44 for another shot at sinking Gill.**

Kim, Ron, and Rufus decide to unleash their powers as one. Together they'll be able to defeat the Ice Queen. Lightning flares as fists fly—but it turns out to be the wrong decision. The Ice Queen freezes all three combatants the moment they touch her.

Humiliation nation. Kim Possible is now Kim Popsicle.

The frozen Kim, Ron, and Rufus are carted away and put in deep freeze until Jackie decides to free them.

👎 **So not the drama! Turn to page 7 to try your luck against Jackie the Jackal again.**

Kim gets Ron to Bueno Nacho—and they learn that the judging for the hot-sauce contest has ended.

"Are you going to be okay?" asks Kim.

Nodding dejectedly, Ron pulls out the vial that contained his entry to the contest. Only a few drops remain anyway. He makes a naco and puts the rest of his sauce on it. The judge rushes over, excited by the rich, spicy aroma,

 and snatches the naco from Ron. The judge takes one bite and declares an upset, presenting the award for best sauce to Ron.

"Woo-chow!" hollers Ron happily, reveling in his new title: Hot Sauce Champion of the World.

👍 **Congratulations! You just helped Kim, Ron, and Rufus save the world from the Masters of Mayhem.**

*K*im decides to challenge the girls to a fashion slam. She thinks her chances of winning are pretty good. She does shop at Club Banana, after all.

"A fashion slam?" cries Lisa. "What's wrong with this picture? You're not even wearing the band's trademark colors or styles."

"Yeah," Millie chimes in. "That outfit is so five minutes ago. But don't worry, we're going to help you out." She summons some other fans.

Kim, Ron, and Rufus are soon surrounded by girls who are eager to give them a makeover—Romeo Five–style. Kim's protective sunglasses are removed and someone hands her a shirt from the concert. Ron and Rufus get the same treatment.

Without her gear, the beat overwhelms Kim. She starts to dance, happily under the band's control.

Mayhem rules—and Dementor wins.

☞ **No big! Turn to page 74 to test Professor Dementor again.**

"**R**on, can you take the wheel for a sec?" Kim asks her pal.

Ron takes over and soon they've dodged all the lava. "Boo-ya!" he shouts.

"Time to let a little air out of Ed's tires," Kim says as she uses her mini–laser wristwatch to burn a hole in one of the Road Hog's tires. But Motor Ed must have planned for tire trouble. The Road Hog is able to ride on its rims.

Then, all of a sudden, Ron leaps from the Smart Car to the Road Hog. A section in the back of the Hog has been damaged and a bunch of crazy colored wires and flashing lights are exposed.

"If I rip out these wires, K.P., I should be able to shut down the Road Hog," Ron says.

Motor Ed tells him, "No, seriously, dude, do that and we'll all be in a world of hurt. Seriously!"

🌐 **Turn to page 38 for Ron to rip out the wires.**

🌐 **Turn to page 66 for Ron to listen to Motor Ed.**

Kim, Ron, and Rufus follow Johnny down a secret corridor.

"I hooked up with a group of the fish scientists who want to rebel against Gill," explains Johnny. "But they need a leader. Knowing Kim Possible's here will convince them to take Gill on!"

Ron notices a group of strange symbols along the corridor that remind him of Gill's scribblings from camp.

"Kim, I think we should go this way." Ron points. "These markings will take us right to Gill!"

"But the fish scientists are this way," Johnny says as he points in the other direction.

🌐 **Turn to page 18 if Kim should follow Johnny.**

🌐 **Turn to page 34 if Kim should follow Ron.**

*T*he trio walks to the end of the tunnel and opens a door to an ancient temple. After a few minutes, they come to a huge room filled with gymnastic equipment.

The cameras appear, and they hear Jackie say, "Tremble in terror as you face the onslaught of the Incredible Bouncing Budd."

Above them, a big round guy in a blue-and-white jumpsuit bounces around. He looks like an enormous beach ball!

"*So* not trembling," yawns Kim.

Suddenly, Bouncing Budd launches himself at the trio like a supersonic dodgeball—and mows them down with ease, steamrolling over them again and again.

Turn to the next page.

"Still not trembling, but definitely spin-ning," Kim moans.

Bouncing Budd moves too quickly for Kim to snag him with her lightning bolts or for Ron to land a solid blow.

"This is *way* too much like gym class," moans Ron.

Two strategies for defeating their opponent bound into Kim's head as Bouncing Budd comes flying at them again. But which should she choose?

🌐 **Turn to page 43 if Kim should try to make a net out of lightning.**

🌐 **Turn to page 68 if Kim should send a lightning strike at Roundhouse Ron to propel him at Budd.**

"*T*hanks for your help, guys," Kim says to Ron and Rufus as she hits the passenger auto-eject button. The roof rolls back, and Ron and Rufus are jettisoned high into the air. They quickly pull their parachutes open and drift toward the ground.

Meanwhile, Kim races alongside the Possible minivan. Whirling grapplers shoot out from the side of the Smart Car and seize hold of the minivan.

"Hang on!" Kim cries as she notices the bridge getting closer. She arcs the Smart Car to the right, so it smashes sidelong into a concrete wall. Just before impact, she blasts to safety with her jetpack. The Smart Car folds up like an accordion as it shudders to a stop. Since the Possibles' car was attached to the now motionless Smart Car, it screeches to a stop, too.

"That was badical!" proclaim the Tweebs. Her family is saved, but Kim now has no chance to stop Ed.

👎 No big! Turn to page 23 for another chance to put the brakes on Motor Ed.

Ron manages to slip from Gill's slimy grasp just as Kim comes charging over to help.

"See, Stoppable?" says Gill. "Even your best friend doesn't think you can take care of yourself. Reminds me of that time at camp . . ."

Realizing her mistake, Kim puts on the brakes and turns back, but it is too late. Gill has a remote control. The lab shakes and shudders as the rocket launches.

Gill's minions easily capture the stunned Kim, Ron, and Rufus.

"Looks like I'm the one who got away," Gill giggles. "And now the whole world is mine!"

☞ **Turn to page 44 for another shot at landing Gill.**

Kim aims her grappling gun carefully. She noticed a weakness in the power grid and is certain that if she hits it just right with the grappler, she can short-circuit it and defeat Dementor.

A Pop Ninja leaps at her. Kim takes her shot with the grappling gun—and misses. The Pop Ninja lands, knocking away Kim's protective glasses and ear gear with a powerful punch.

"Rude much?" asks Kim, holding her jaw. Without the gear, the band's message of mayhem suddenly makes perfect sense to Kim. She snatches Ron's and Rufus's gear, and all three join the other mind-controlled teens as they surge from the concert hall to spread chaos everywhere!

☞ **Turn to page 74 to try to send the professor back to school.**

*R*on hesitates—giving Kim a chance to leap onto the Road Hog with him. Kim smells something bad and quickly realizes that it's not just Motor Ed's stinky aftershave. The Road Hog is acting like a real pig, using the exhaust from the other cars on the highway as its fuel source. Kim signals Wade with the revelation. The authorities patch through to the car manufacturers, who tell them to  use a special satellite signal that will cause the computers in the cars to shut down.

In moments, Motor Ed's Road Hog starts to slow. He knows that he's in trouble—so he sets his sights on the Smart Car, which has energy cells that might help him achieve his goal.

🌐 **Turn to page 33 if Kim should drive the Smart Car to safety.**

🌐 **Turn to page 70 if Kim should let Motor Ed use the Smart Car's energy cells, in case they overload the Road Hog.**

Kim grabs the Kimmunicator. "Wade, I need some overload codes, superfast."

Wade clicks away on his keyboard and sends the codes to Kim just five seconds later.

Kim punches them in.

An electronic voice announces, "Rocket launch aborted."

The Kimmunicator beeps again. Kim glances at Ron, who's barely hanging on. She pulls Gill away.

Meanwhile, Wade has been giving Rufus instructions via the Kimmunicator. The mole rat punches in more codes on the control panel and hits a button. Suddenly, all the mutations are reversed.

Even Gill is human again. The Fish Patrol changes back to young scientists and activates a control that makes the compound rise to the surface, where the authorities take Gill into custody.

"Come on, we gotta book!" calls Ron. "The Bueno Nacho sauce contest waits for no man."

👍 **You win! If you've defeated all the villains, turn to page 57.**

👍 **To pick a new villain, turn to page 5.**

Kim points at Ron and a lightning bolt sends him flying at Budd. He smacks the wall with explosive force—and hears a terrible rumbling. Huge cracks open in the walls and ceiling. Kim looks over sharply as the floor quakes and moans. "Ron?"

"Uh . . . it wasn't me?" moans Ron weakly.

Budd rushes to a secret exit and makes his escape—as the entire temple comes crashing down! Luckily Kim, Ron, and Rufus didn't get hit with anything. But when the dust settles, they find themselves trapped in the wreckage. Jackie appears in a holograph to tell them he'll rescue them soon . . . after he's conquered the world with his show! Way harsh!

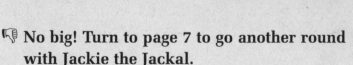

👎 **No big! Turn to page 7 to go another round with Jackie the Jackal.**

"**I** challenge you to a dance-off," Kim tells the angry mob. The fans huddle for a minute, then the leader, a tall girl in leather pants, agrees.

"Wait, K.P.," Ron says. "I've got something that will make our moves sizzle." He holds up a bottle of his special sauce.

Kim, Ron, and Rufus taste a few drops each—and their mouths burn so badly that they yelp and whirl and dance like dervishes.

Talk about great moves! Those angry fans never had a chance. The crowd bursts into applause—and moves aside so Kim, Ron, and Rufus can get to the band.

🌐 **Turn to page 28 if Kim should cause a ruckus by suggesting one of the boys has a hair out of place.**

🌐 **Turn to page 31 if Kim should have Ron signal Wade for backup while she rumbles with the Romeos.**

Motor Ed snags the Smart Car's energy cells and jams them into the Road Hog. But his vehicle doesn't know how to handle this much direct energy. It grows bigger and bigger, literally hogging the entire road, until it becomes so bloated and heavy that it can't move at all.

"Stoppable rules!" cries Ron. "You snooze, you lose!"

Ed's plans are ruined—and help quickly arrives to get Kim, her family, Ron, and Rufus to the sauce contest—just in time!

👍 **You win! If you've defeated all the villains, turn to page 57.**

👍 **To pick a new villain, turn to page 5.**

Kim chooses Bast and Nast to help her fight Jackie. The cat-women are terrific in the ring. Jackie is pounded and pummeled into defeat.

Girrrls rule!

"Yo, K.P.," Ron says uneasily, looking over Kim's shoulder. "How come your friends are, uh . . . *glowing*?"

Kim whirls—and is knocked out by a mystical blast.

When Kim wakes up, she and her pals are trapped in a windowless room.

Bast and Nast are magical entities just like Jackie, and with him out of the way, they plan to take over the show—and the world.

"I guess they weren't such cool cats after all," Ron says.

☞ **That's showbiz! Turn to page 7 to try to take down Jackie the Jackal again.**

At the edge of the crowd, Kim uses her souped-up shades to get a closer view of the singers. "Ron, they're all wearing lightweight head-gear like ours, but theirs has Dementor's initials! It must  cause them to do whatever Dementor tells them. If we can reach the Romeos and tear off Dementor's shades and earplugs, we should be able to free the crowd!"

"Fantabulous," says Ron. "Let's pay a visit to the band."

But as Kim and Ron try to reach the stage, overprotective, mind-controlled fans crowd around them, blocking their path.

🌐 **Turn to page 14 if Kim should use her flash-weapon/compact and sonar shades to get to the band.**

🌐 **Turn to page 69 if Kim should challenge the fans to a dance-off to prove she's one of them.**

Kim, Ron, and Rufus navigate the maze. Cameras appear—along with a young guy wearing purple-and-white spandex, who walks through the wall like a ghost.

"Call me the 4-D Dude," he says.

Kim's lightning bolts and Ron's roundhouse punches pass through him harmlessly.

"Hey, no fair!" shouts Ron.

4-D darts in and out of walls, foiling Kim and Ron's attempts to stop him. Then he becomes solid and smacks Ron, announcing, "I'm superdense."

"I wouldn't be too proud of that," Ron remarks.

🌐 Turn to page 15 to let Rufus make a desperate run at 4-D.

🌐 Turn to page 30 if Kim should use her boomerang hair comb so Ron can lay the hurt on 4-D.

PROFESSOR DEMENTOR

"**A** concert?" cries the totally tweaked Ron as he stands outside a concert arena with Kim and Rufus. The mad bass lines of the world-famous boy band Romeo Five are thundering from within. "But the Masters of Mayhem have to be stopped. And we've got to get to the sauce contest."

"Wade says there have been outbreaks of people going completely wacky, creating, well, *mayhem* all over the world for the past few weeks," Kim explains. "Entire towns have been devastated. After a while the people seem to snap out of it, but they have no idea why they've been so destructive."

Kim puts on the coolest pair of shades ever and hands matching glasses to Ron and Rufus. "Wade's been working on this for a while," she

74

Go to the next page.

goes on, "and he finally linked all the incidents to a weird signal. This signal is like the one that Professor Dementor has been developing for his mind-control research."

"Mind control," says Ron. "So Dementor's behind this. Most twisted."

"*Uh-huh*," agrees Rufus.

"And that signal is coming out of the concert dome even as we speak," Kim says, adjusting her shades. A set of earphones springs out and settles into place. She hands out slim silver boxes. "This looks like an MP3 player, but it's really a supercomputer that's working with our shades and headphones to protect us. Wade totally rules."

They go inside, breezing past a handful of beefy guys who should be working the doors but are more interested in playing video games. "I had a feeling they weren't going to ask for tickets," Kim confesses. "The mayhem signal is already working."

Inside, rows of screaming teens reach toward the stage, where the incredibly handsome band members are singing and

Turn to the next page.

dancing. The band invites a pair of teens onstage and has them sing along.

"'No more school! No more rules!'" they bellow. "'Keep it real our way, don't be fools.'"

"Sheesh!" says Ron. "I didn't think these guys had such serious 'tude."

Then the band commands the girls to stand on their heads and keep singing. And then the band changes up their lyrics, demanding the teens throughout the audience pledge to fight as their soldiers.

"Vive la révolution! Chaos in the street!" they chant. "Mayhem rules, yo! We can't be beat!"

The crowd explodes with cheers. Dementor's using the band to spread his message of mayhem! What's Kim to do?

🌐 **Turn to page 42 to send Kim backstage in her quest to find Professor Dementor.**

🌐 **Turn to page 51 if Kim should climb the rigging above to shut down the power.**

🌐 **Turn to page 72 if Kim should plunge through the crowd and take on the band directly.**

*K*im, Ron, and Rufus swim into the darkness. The farther they go, the deeper the water gets. The water pressure is too much for the hammerheads. Fortunately, Kim, Ron, and Rufus are protected by their high-tech diving suits. They double back, past the now-sleeping hammerheads, and sneak into the complex undetected.

Once inside, Ron turns to Kim and says, "We should try out the image-transforming thingies."

Kim frowns. "I'm still not sure we can trust those science-camp kids. Let's wait and use the distorters only if we have to."

Kim, Ron, and Rufus prowl through the compound's high-ceilinged chambers and narrow silver-metal corridors. They pass control panels pulsing with green, blue, and amber lights. After a few minutes of spying on Gill's dull-eyed, 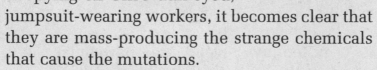 jumpsuit-wearing workers, it becomes clear that they are mass-producing the strange chemicals that cause the mutations.

Suddenly, the wall behind Kim, Ron, and

Turn to the next page.

Rufus slides open to reveal the Fish Patrol, a group of armor-plated, muscular fish-mutants who guard the compound.

"Too late to use the image thingie, huh?" asks Ron.

" 'Fraid so," replies Kim.

She launches herself at the startled fish guards, knocking out three of them with high kicks and open-palm strikes. But even with Ron and Rufus's help, the friends are quickly overwhelmed.

Just as a scaly guard is about to throw a net over Kim, Ron, and Rufus, a cry from behind the patrol makes them whirl. A handsome young guy with black hair and sparkling blue eyes springs into action. He attacks the Fish Patrol, his hands and fists moving with blinding speed.

The fish go down.

"I'm Johnny Seven," the newcomer says, standing atop a heap of moaning mackerel-men.

Go to the next page.

"I work for a spy service that has the same interests as you: stopping Gill and saving the planet."

"Which service?" asks Kim.

Johnny shrugs. "Sorry. Classified."

The Fish Patrol is vanquished, but the place is crawling with Gill's mutants.

"Follow me!" Johnny calls, pointing at the entrance to a secret series of corridors.

🌐 **Turn to page 39 for Kim to duck into the abandoned room up ahead.**

🌐 **Turn to page 60 if Kim should follow Johnny.**

Don't miss Kim's next "PicK a ViLLaiN!" adventure!

For Kim Possible, being a teen super-hero is so not the drama. But when four of her archenemies rob the Global Bank, she's got to decide who to take on first: Aviarius, Falsetto Jones, Frugal Lucre, or White Stripe? It's a Kim Possible adventure where you make the choices— win or lose!